10/50

I Can Do It All By Myself
books by
Shigeo Watanabe

**How do I put it on?**
AN AMERICAN LIBRARY ASSOCIATION
NOTABLE CHILDREN'S BOOK

**What a good lunch!**

**Get set! Go!**

**I'm the king of the castle!**

**I can ride it!**

**Where's my daddy?**

**I can build a house!**

**I can take a walk!**

Text copyright © 1981 by Shigeo Watanabe.
Illustrations copyright © 1981 by Yasuo Ohtomo.
American text copyright © 1982 by Philomel Books.
All rights reserved.
Published in the United States by Philomel Books, a division of
The Putnam Publishing Group, 51 Madison Ave., New York, N.Y. 10010.
Printed in the United States.
Library of Congress CIP information at back of book.

# I'm the king of the castle!

Story by Shigeo Watanabe    Pictures by Yasuo Ohtomo

**4**

PLAYING ALONE

PHILOMEL BOOKS

I'm going to play in the sandbox
all by myself.
I'll take my shovel.

I'll need my pail, too.

# This is very hard work.

# What a mountain!

# I'm the king of the castle!

# Now I'll dig a hole.

# A great big hole.

# A very deep hole.

If I fill it up with water . . .

. . . it will make a lake.

# It's nice and muddy.

# I had fun playing all by myself!

Library of Congress Cataloging in Publication Data
Watanabe, Shigeo, 1928-
I'm the king of the castle.
(An I can do it all by myself book) (Playing alone ; #4)
SUMMARY: Using his shovel and pail, Bear constructs
a land where he is king.
[1. Play—Fiction. 2. Bears—Fiction]
1. Ohtomo, Yasuo, ill. II. Title.
PZ7.W2615lm [E] 81-15865
ISBN 0-399-20868-2    AACR2
ISBN 0-399-61195-9 (lib. bdg.)
ISBN 0-399-21045-8 pbk.
First paperback edition published in 1984.
Second impression